Tales of Highwaymen,

OR THE ROMANCE OF THE ROAD.

"FOOL," SAID CAPTAIN HAWK, "IF YOU ARE NOW TAKING YOUR LAST LOOK OF THIS WORLD IT'S NOT MY FAULT."

No. 1

TALES of HIGHWAYMEN;

or, The Romance of the Road.

The Shadow of Death; or, The Coffin Cell.

PROLOGUE.

STANDING under the archway of an ancient inn I gazed upon Newgate.

It was midnight, and I stood alone, musing upon the chronicle of the dismal prison.

I conjured up ghostly visions of beings over whom the grave had closed, and whose faults follies, crimes, and virtues had flowed down the stream of time, and were now unheeded and forgotten.

The night had been serene, but now the wind blew in mournful gusts round the prison ; the sky became of a pitchy darkness, and now and then a strange moaning sound pervaded the air, as if restless spirits were still hovering about the terrible building.

Thus I stood until a faint streak in the eastern sky began to roll back the curtain of night.

But dimly did the grim and gruesome outline of Newgate present itself even now to my eyes.

I could see it, but that was all ; but yet the very dimness of its aspect seemed to conjure up with more distinctness to my mind's eye the dread visions of the past.

"Innocent hearts," I said aloud, "have felt pangs of agony within those walls. The guiltless have been sent to death, and oh ! Newgate, the blood of men murdered in the name of the law cries out aloud for vengeance against thee."

At this moment something touched me, and I started on one side.

"Are you deaf ?" demanded a croaking voice. "Are you deaf. I have spoken twice and had no answer."

Looking down, I saw a miserable object almost at my feet.

It was a diminutive old beggarman, so crippled that he was compelled to use a crutch for support, and it was with that he had touched me.

"Well," he said, "what do you think of me now ? I am a cripple and a beggar. Can you add anything else to my description ? You behaved rudely enough to me. Well, well, what else can such a wretched apology for a man as I expect ?"

"I had no intention of offending you," I replied. "I thought I was alone."

"Humph !" said the cripple. "Did you come here to look at Newgate ? I wonder how many times I have come to look at it by night and by day, in sunshine and in gloom, in calm and storm. What do you know of Newgate ?"

"Nothing ; but in its outer walls I find much food for reflection."

"It is full of facts !" cried the old man. "You spoke of the innocent suffering within these walls. I like the tone in which you spoke. Look at me again. I am hideously ugly. I am wretchedly poor. I don't seem to be formed after Adam. Perhaps I am a little mad. If you are curious about Newgate, you might do worse than to come home with me and pass an hour."

"Willingly."

"That is well," returned the old man, who seemed to be delighted at my acceptance of his invitation. "I like your voice. When I can see your face I will decide upon what more I can do. Perhaps I may give you an admission to Newgate."

"You give me an admission !" I cried. "I thought that power was vested in the sheriffs and a few other City dignitaries."

The old man laughed scornfully.

"The sheriffs show you Newgate !" he cried, striking his crutch against the ground. "They never saw it themselves."

"Indeed. You surprise me."

"Who will show you the old dungeons," the beggarman continued. "Who will guide you through the passages long since given up to myriads of rats and reptiles ? Who will escort you through

the clump of trees from whence he had emerged. The sound of the horse's hoofs upon the snow was completely hushed, as if it trod upon many folds of velvet, and then all was still for a few minutes.

Even then but faintly could be heard the beat of a horse's hoofs at a canter, but when the sound had once broken upon the stillness it momentarily increased until it was clear and evident that some mounted man was about to pass close to the ambuscade.

And now with a *sang froid* that was one of the remarkable characteristics of the highwayman he trotted out from his place of concealment, and whistling a popular air of the day, placed himself in such a position in the way of the advancing stranger as made it evident he meant to intercept him.

He who was coming on at so good a pace seemed to be at once aware that he would not be allowed to pass so readily that little clump of wood as he had at first supposed.

He reined in his steed, and advanced at a walking pace.

When he got so near to the highwayman that it required no exertion of voice to make anything heard upon either side the latter spoke.

"Hilloa! sir traveller, whither so fast?" cried the highwayman. "We collect a toll here, and we leave it to the generosity of a gentleman to make it worth our while to keep the gate."

"What do you mean by that?" demanded the stranger; "are you mad or drunk?"

"Neither, my good sir; but if you must have it in plainer language, I have a difficulty in telling the right time of day, and therefore will trouble you for your watch. I admire jewellery, and if you have any, will wear it for your sake. Dame Fortune has jilted me at cards—I will revenge myself for her frowns by levying a contribution from you; and if that won't do, why, have it shorter or plainer still—your money or your life!"

"A highwayman!" said the stranger. "Tell me one thing before I punish this insolence as it deserves. Are you Captain Hawk, who is sometimes called the Double Knight, in consequence of the rapidity of your movements from place to place?"

"Most devotedly at your service," said the highwayman, and he slightly lifted the hat from his head. "I admire your delicacy; you would not be robbed by a lesser hand than mine."

"I'm afraid," said the stranger, "I shall scarcely merit your thanks; I asked you who you were, in order that I might be quite sure that I was ridding Society of one of its greatest pests; and as I am about to make a sojourn in the neighbourhood, it's as well that I should commence by ridding it of you."

The young man—for young he was—uttered those words with rapidity, and while the last were upon his lips, he drew from his saddle a pistol, and fired it at the head of the highwayman.

The report in the dense cool air was loud and clear, and it appeared absolutely impossible that the knight of the road could have escaped the shot.

"That was well meant," said Captain Hawk, as his horse reared, and he had some difficulty to bring him round again.

"And have I missed him?' said the young man. "Confusion!"

"It's my turn now," said the highwayman.

He at once fired upon his adversary, and with a better aim, for the young man reeled and fell from the saddle.

Captain Hawk was close to him in a moment.

"Fool!" he said, "if you are now taking your last look of this world it's not my fault. I would have spared you if I could."

With professional dexterity he helped himself to the valuables the young man had about him, consisting of a watch, a considerable sum of money, and some papers which, although of no intrinsic value in themselves, were so mingled with the cash that the highwayman took all together, without taking the trouble to separate them.

"Scoundrel!" muttered the young stranger, between his clenched teeth. "I am badly hurt, but we shall meet again."

"I will hope for that pleasure," said the highwayman; "and when we do meet again be a little more careful of your mode of reception. I bear a charmed life. Adieu!"

CHAPTER III.

THE OXFORD MAIL.

HUMMING an air, Captain Hawk, with all the nonchalance in the world, turned his horse's head and trotted gently from the spot.

"To be robbed," said the wounded man, "robbed on the highway by one man. How faint I am—I cannot raise my arm, and I can feel the blood pouring from the finger-ends of my glove, and there he goes in triumph. Yet, no. Why should he? I have another weapon here; there may be virtue in a second bullet; 'tis not a long shot, and I have hit my mark at a far greater distance. If—if, now, I could but bring him down."

With his left hand—for it was his right arm that had been broken by the shot of the highwayman—he drew his second pistol from its saddle-case, and taking as steady an aim as he could he fired after the retreating horseman.

In an instant the highwayman wheeled round and came back to him.

"Ratchley Boyes," he said, "I know you. For this second shot, I owe you an everlasting grudge. I will not pay you now, because the score will keep; but remember that the Hawk owes you one, and pay-day always comes. There's your bullet."

He thrust into the hands of the bewildered young man a leaden bullet and then, clapping spurs to his horse, galloped at a hard pace from the spot.

Bewildered by the singularity of the adventure and exhausted with the loss of blood, young Ratchley Boyes felt a film gather over his eyes.

And then came darkness and oblivion.

His horse seemed to know that something fearful was amiss.

It threw up its head, snorted, and pawed the ground for a minute or two, then with a sudden plunge darted furiously and wildly across the heath, while the blood of its rider was changing the hue of the snow about him.

.   .   .   .   .   .

"Main cold, ain't it? Them as is at home is best off. Be yer got any toes, neighbour?"

These words were uttered by a rough country-man at the top of the Oxford mail to a shivering passenger who sat beside him, and who only vouchsafed to say in reply, in a sulky tone—

"Don't bother."

"Well!" said the countryman, "I do say it be main cold. It's enough to take the nose off a stone statue. What do you say, marm? How do you feel?"

"I haven't had any feeling for ever so long," replied a voice from a huddled up mass of clothing. "Ugh! And they tell me that the monster who calls himself Captain Hawk is in the neighbourhood."

"Oh! it be too cold to be robbed on such a night as this," the farmer returned. "Hawk is a good judge of creature comforts, and I'll be bound that he is warming his thieving carcase over some inn fire. I say, mister, how do you like this sort o' weather?"

"Confound you!" muttered the man addressed. "Don't keep punching me in the ribs in that way. I tell you I am too cold to talk, so don't bother me."

"Good gracious!" cried the lady, "how the coach is swaying to and fro."

"Hullo there!" shouted the guard to the coach-man, "where are you going to? I'll bet a guinea that we are off the road?"

"Who the deuce can see the road?" retorted the coachman with a growl. "It's all the same for miles round. Bust my buttons if I shall know Hounslow Heath when I see it!"

The coachman had to be extremely careful with the reins now.

The ponderous vehicle had evidently strayed from the highroad, and now and then lurched and rolled so ominously as the wheels sank into deep ruts that the alarm of the passengers momentarily increased.

The poor horses, panting with fatigue, struggled bravely on, until one went down in the snow.

"Hold hard," said the guard. "There's some-body on horseback coming, and perhaps he can tell us where we are going to."

"There be no hurry now that one of the bits of cattle is down," grumbled the coachman. "I see the man. I think we are in the right path, but the stranger is coming exactly in our line, and whistling away as if he is as warm as a toast."

"Hallo there!" cried the guard, as the horseman trotted carelessly up to the coach.

"Can you tell us where we are?"

"Yes!" replied the stranger, doffing his hat. "You are on Hounslow Heath. You'll want a good story to tell when you get to the inn to-night,

and you can say that you were stopped by Captain Hawk."

The female passenger outside gave a loud shriek, rousing a lady within who took up the key note and responded with a long succession of screams.

"Hush!" said the guard as he prepared a huge bell-mouthed blunderbuss for action. "I'll have him. Don't speak—don't breathe—I'll have him. Now for a nob scuttler."

Click went the lock, but no explosion took place.

"Why, you fool," said the man who objected to be disturbed, "it's been snowing into the barrel of that waterspout of yours for the last two hours and a-half."

"Lor!" gasped the guard. "My eye! who'd a thought o' that," and he looked carefully into the barrel of the blunderbuss. "Well, all I have to say is if it had gone off it would have made mince-meat of him. There's two pennorth of iron tacks in this ere weapon, besides a dozen lumps of lead."

Whether the highwayman calculated upon the disabled state of the guard's blunderbuss it is difficult to say, but he certainly took no notice of it.

"I said I would stop the Oxford coach," he observed, coolly, "and I have kept my word. You, Tom Brown, driver of the coach, attend me. I'll lodge a couple of bullets amongst your fat if you move from the box, so don't be a fool."

Captain Hawk then rode to the coach door, and in a moment he saw that no effectual opposition would be offered him from those within.

"Gentlemen," he said, "you will be so kind as to hand me anything valuable you may have about you. Ladies, your contributions will be thankfully received, but if there be any little article you wish to preserve, pray do so."

"He's a nice man, mamma," said a young lady, who was in the extreme corner of the coach.

"Hold your tongue, you hussy," cried the mother; "how dare you speak!"

"Have mercy upon us, sir," said a young gentle-man, who had been amusing the passengers for the last twenty miles with anecdotes of his feats of courage. "Have mercy upon us, dear sir, if you please. I have a tender parent, sir. I'm only nineteen, sir. Take everything, but don't hurt us."

Rings, watches, and purses were handed toler-ably freely.

The highwayman's policy was always to take as much as he could, and as quickly as possible, but the appeal of the young gentleman appeared to ex-cite his indignation.

"Why, you ape in boy's clothes," he said, "hand over your purse, and keep quiet."

"Oh! no; oh! no—no—no! Don't, Mr. Highwayman, don't; think of my mother!"

The whole of the scene did not take more than a few minutes to bring to a conclusion.

"You can go on all, and good night," said Captain Hawk. "Tom Brown, don't boast at the Swan again that you've never been robbed."

He was about to move off, when most unexpectedly two stalwart men, who had descended from the roof of the coach, seized his horse's bridle.

"Hurrah! hurrah!" cried the guard. "Nabbed him at last."

A blow on the head from a heavy butt-end of a pistol released the highwayman from one of his assailants, who instantly dropped, but the other clung to him with such desperate tenacity that he was compelled, from the bounds of the horse, and the manner in which he was held, to release his feet from the stirrups, and slip from the saddle.

The struggle on foot was short and decisive.

The highwayman gave his opponent a terrific fall, and then, as fast as he could through the snow, he strove to recall his horse, which had bounded off to some distance.

"He's afoot now!—he's afoot now, Tom," cried the guard. "Hurrah! after him."

"Here goes," said the fat coachman, pulling up the fallen horse by sheer force, "and blow everything!"

He turned his horses' heads in the direction the highwayman had taken, and for about half a minute there was the phenomenon of a coach and four horses pursuing a man; then there was a heavy lurch of the cumbrous vehicle, loud shrieks rent the air, and over went the Oxford coach into a snow-drift.

Captain Hawk had caught his horse and sprung into the saddle. A glance showed him the state of affairs as regarded the Oxford mail, and with a loud ringing laugh he pushed his horse at full speed towards it.

A tremendous leap cleared the whole obstruction, and before anyone dared to look up for fear of the horse's heels, he was out of sight.

CHAPTER IV.

THE HIGHWAYMAN'S HOME.

THE occurrences which we have related are not of a nature to be without their serious consequences.

The very sound of the name of so redoubted a highwayman as Captain Hawk was at any time sufficient to produce a large amount of consternation in any district.

His reputation extended over every county in England, although the most daring of his depredations were usually committed in the neighbourhood of the metropolis.

There can be no doubt that rumour and popular exaggeration had done much more for the fame of this redoubtable highwayman than he had ever done himself; but, notwithstanding all this, and that a great many feats of skill and valour were attributed to him which he never dreamed of performing, he was a man of no mean accomplishments.

After the two perilous adventures in which he had been engaged, Captain Hawk sped on at a speed that showed he had still something on his mind.

In his attack upon Ratchley Boyes he had been deliberate and calm, and his attack upon the Oxford coach had been conducted as if he had ample time at his disposal.

The country into which the highwayman now plunged was overgrown with thick brushwood, and interspersed with tall trees.

With an intimate knowledge of the locality Hawk threaded his way onwards through a wood.

The thick branches of the trees hung close to the ground, and the place assumed all the appearance of a preserve, expressly so thickly planted in order that it might become a cover for game.

Without a moment's consideration, but as if he had arrived at some particular spot at which it had been his fixed intention, Captain Hawk flung himself from his horse, and, drawing the bridle over the animal's head, he tied it to the stump of a tree.

Speaking a word of friendly admonition to the creature, he proceeded forward or foot, through a tangled mass of vegetation which a horseman could not have hoped to thread.

The boughs under which he walked produced a darkness beneath them almost as intense as if they had been clothed in all the beauty of their summer foliage; for so interlaced had they become that the snowflakes falling thickly upon them had, in many instances, filled up the small interstices, producing all the appearances of a thatch of spotless whiteness above, but, underneath, as dark as Erebus.

Suddenly he emerged on to a clear space, and then a few steps brought him to the door of a small hovel, which, standing as it did in that waste of nature, shut out apparently from all companionship with civilisation, must surely, if inhabited at all, be the home of some person of most singular tastes and habits.

It was evident that Captain Hawk presumed upon finding somebody to welcome him, even in that wretched lonely hut; and it would appear, too, that he judged but a slight summons would be sufficient to announce his presence.

He gave the door a tap with his hand, saying at the same moment—

"Time—time!"

There was a flash of light from a wretched-looking casement.

The low growl of a dog, and then the door was flung open, and a man with a small lantern in his hand appeared, holding by the collar a strange mongrel-looking cur, which seemed ready at once to dart upon the intruder.

"Ah! captain," said the man. "Beauty only heard the knock, and not your voice, or she wouldn't show her teeth in this way. You are welcome. Walk in, captain. Any luck, to-night?"

"What have you to do with that?" Hawk replied ungraciously, as he strode across the threshold. "And as for being welcome, it would be hard indeed if a man were not so at his own home."

"So it would—so it would," said the other, nodding his head. "What about the Oxford mail, captain?"

"Stopped," Hawk replied, curtly.

"Eh—what?"

"Stopped, I tell you, and left in a snowdrift."

The man put down the lantern and burst into a roar of laughter.

"Confound you! I have no time for your folly," Captain Hawk hissed. "How is she? Better or worse—alive or dead?"

"Raving away as usual," the man replied, "and singing the old songs over again."

"The old songs, eh?" muttered the captain. "Take care of these things until I return. And, look you, keep a sharp eye upon her. If she escapes, you shall rue the day that you were born. Stay here, and venture not out until you see me again. Show no light at night, and be as cautious as a fox. Remember that I shall be in the neighbourhood, and have a keen sight. Here, give me the lantern."

As he spoke, Captain Hawk divested himself of his scarlet coat and flung it on the floor of the hut.

He then took off his hat and his horseman's boots, and snatching the lantern from the hands of the man, he opened a door, and passing through, closed it after him.

"Hullo! captain," cried the man, who did not seem to relish being left in the dark. "Captain, I say."

The door opened, and Captain Hawk reappeared.

"What now?" he cried, sternly. "What are you bellowing at, idiot that you are?"

"I only asked you not to blow out the light," the man mumbled through his teeth.

"Hush! What's that?"

The fellow pointed with his forefinger to the ceiling of the hut.

"It's her—her above," he replied. "I thought you would hear something of her before you went. That's the way she goes on night and day. A nice sort of life this is for a man to lead—keeper to a madwoman. There she goes again, and all her talk is about—"

"What?" demanded Captain Hawk.

"Newgate."

Just then a strange, half-smothered wailing of a female voice came from above.

"Innocent—innocent!" she cried. "I tell you again and again that I am innocent. Such a deed were too dreadful to think of. Oh! horror. This is Newgate—Newgate—Newgate, the home of despair, the sepulchre in which hope lies buried for ever. Newgate! Why am I here? I did not do it, I never saw its eyes, it never looked upon me. Help—help—help!"

"There's a yell," said the man. "Captain, did you hear that? That is what I have to listen to times out of number. I say, can you give me an idea how long it is to last? It's out of my line, this keeper business."

Captain Hawk said not a word; but very slowly, as if he feared to make the least noise, he closed the door again, which separated the two lower apartments of the hut.

"Well," said the man, whom he had now again left in the dark, "I can't say as I knows the rights of it, but the captain does, I suppose. He said he was afraid she'd lay violent hands on her-self. No such luck, say I; 'twas but yesterday I chucked her an old piece of rope and a gimlet, just to give her a chance of hanging herself, but it was no go. I say, captain—what an odd fish he is! I'll be hanged if he ain't gone—he's popped out by the other way—and now I hear the sound of his horse's feet. There can be no mistake about it. If he's put out the light now, I'd just as soon be hung at once."

The supposition that Captain Hawk had left the hut was perfectly correct.

Probably he had only come there to effect one of those remarkable changes of costume at which he had such surprising tact; but certain it is he was off, whatever had been his object, and in a few moments the sound of his horse's feet had died away upon the night air.

All was still again and as the grave, save an occasional low moaning wail from that heart-stricken creature in the loft, and the muttered curses of the man, who seemed half inclined to defy, and yet to dread doing so, the orders of Captain Hawk to remain where he was as a sentinel over that luckless and ill starred woman.

In the meantime, how or by what means the dog belonging to the Boyes family had found the glove saturated with the gore of young Ratchley, no one knew.

Possibly, having accompanied the remainder of the family to the farmhouse, and not being considered a fit guest for the well-filled ball-room of the Talbot, he had taken, of his own accord, a stroll upon the heath, and the scent of blood might have taken him to the spot where the young man had met with his misadventure.

We cannot say that this fortunate finding of the glove was the means of saving the life of Ratchley Boyes, for although he had now fainted from exhaustion, where he lay, the intense cold of the night and the still falling snow, prevented the further effusion of blood from his wound.

But still, he might have been subject to other accidents but for the timely aid which came to him in consequence of the discovery.

We left our guests at the Talbot in a state of the greatest apprehension and alarm.

May Boyes was quickly taken from the arms of Gerald Clifton, and consigned to the guardianship of the portly Mrs. Butts, who, folding her in an embrace that perfectly extinguished her, called out for water, as the poor girl had fainted.

"And the poor thing," said Peter Butts, "will be suffocated too, if you don't let her go. For Heaven's sake, wife, set her down. It's like being embraced by a state bed, with full chintz hangings."

"My dear Sir John," said Gerald Clifton, "let my feelings of friendship for your family, and admiration for yourself, plead my excuse for being so rude as to request to know really what is the matter."

"Ratchley—Ratchley!" exclaimed May, who had now sufficiently recovered to hear and understand what was going on around her. "Where is Ratchley? Gerald Clifton, where is he? Came he not with you?"

Tales of Highwaymen,

OR THE ROMANCE OF THE ROAD.

"CAPTAIN HAWK!" GASPED THE TOLL-KEEPER. "WHY—WHY, THERE'S A TREMENDOUS HUE AND CRY AFTER YOU."

"A great part of the way he certainly did. We separated some few miles off. I had a call to make, and we took separate routes."

"Oh! seek him—seek him; he is murdered!" cried May.

"Lights—lights! my masters," cried Peter Butts. "The dog hasn't come far, I'll be bound, and if young Master Ratchley has met with any accident you may depend it's on the heath. We'll soon find him. Cheer up, Miss May; a little blood makes a great show; and, after all, if this be Master Ratchley's glove, he may not be much hurt. Come on—come on! We'll have a hunt for him in the snow. Lay hold of all the candles you can, my men, and follow me."

"And how many candles," said Gerald Clifton, "do you expect will live out-of-doors on such a night as this? A stable lantern will answer all the purpose; and yonder dog, no doubt, will guide you to the spot where any mischief lies."

"Will you come with us, sir?"

"Most certainly. Bear with me a moment, and I'm with you."

He stooped till his lips touched the ear of May Boyes.

"Be not alarmed," he said; "always sufficient for the hour is its evil. I love Ratchley for his sake, as well for the sake of one whom I love better. I will not return to you without news of him. Adieu! dear May; let me live in your remembrance."

Before May Boyes could return to him even a word of thanks he was gone, but his words had filled her with a strange and new delight.

Did she love Gerald Clifton? She had not yet asked the question of her own heart. Had she asked it, she would have feared to reply to it; and yet truthfulness was an inherent principle in the mind of May Boyes. What was it, then, in a few and simple words Gerald Clifton had uttered which brought so exquisite a sensation of pleasure to her heart?

Fifty willing hands were ready to do any good service for May Boyes.

Peter Butts had no want of assistance in the search he proposed upon the snow-clad heath, and the large, thronged room in the old Talbot Inn, which had so lately appeared crammed almost to uneasiness with guests, wore a deserted aspect, while the ruddy glares from the fires within the house shone forth now from the open doors and casements; for those who went not forth for the search followed with straining eyes those who did, as they saw them, like black specks upon the snow, following the track of the dog, who now bounded on towards the spot where Ratchley Boyes lay in the seeming sleep of death.

They sped forward to render every assistance that might be required, and when the dog suddenly paused and set up a lengthened howl, old Peter Butts, who was foremost, stepped forward but another pace, and then held his lantern to the ground, as he exclaimed—

"Good Heaven! my masters, he is, indeed, murdered. Here's a sight! Heaven help us all."

There lay Ratchley in the midst of such a mass of snow and blood that it was terrible to look upon him; and although the throng of persons, impelled by intense curiosity, first crowded closely round what they supposed to be the body, a kind of terror soon fell upon them, and with one accord they shrank back, making a wider circle round that fearful spectacle.

Gerald Clifton without a word snatched the lantern from the landlord's hand, and regardless of the half-frozen pool of blood around, he flung himself upon one knee by the body, and, tearing open the vest, he astonished everyone by placing his ear flat upon the region of the heart, as if he were intent upon nestling on the bosom of the dead.

It was but for an instant he remained in that attitude.

"He lives!" he cried. "And, if I may judge from his appearance, he is not much hurt. Carry him at once to the inn. He is insensible, but when there we shall soon hear from his own lips some account of what has reduced him to this condition."

This assertion, spoken so confidently, exercised an effect quite magical upon all present. The strange solemnity and the awe-struck appearance that had sat upon every countenance while they thought that they were in the presence of death immediately fled, and many who probably could not have been induced by any bribe to touch the dead body, now that they believed life only for a time suspended, were the most eager in rendering efficient assistance in the conveyance of the wounded man to a place of safety.

Poor Ratchley had become completely frozen to the ground, and it required an effort to disengage his apparel from the earth and snow.

Four persons lifted him in their arms, and Gerald Clifton, leading the way with the lantern, and taking rapid strides along the same path they had so lately traversed, they all proceeded with their ghastly burden with far greater speed than they had left the inn.

When they arrived within sight of its time-hallowed porch, Gerald Clifton handed the lantern to the landlord, and then dashed forward alone with great speed, so that he reached the dancing-room some minutes before those who carried the wounded man.

He dashed in without the slightest ceremony or preparation.

"He lives—he lives!" he cried; "Ratchley lives. He is but slightly hurt. May Boyes—where is she?"

"He lives!" cried Sir John, and thought he was sinking into a chair, but in reality fell on the floor. "Lives! then the baronetcy will not be extinct, and the glory of the Boyes will yet continue unfaded."

"Where is May?" demanded Gerald.

"Young sir," said Sir John, "there ought to have been a chair behind me—some miscreant has removed it; and as for my daughter, the Lady May, she is in a chamber precisely above this room, as I am informed, carefully tended by—"

"Thank you—thank you!" said Gerald, and,

turning upon his heel, he dashed from the ballroom and up the first staircase that presented itself.

"Confound these old rambling places !" he said, hesitating ; "one cannot guess which way to turn. Sir John mentioned the room immediately above the hall. Ah ! I hear the sound of voices ; that must be the room ; the news I bring sanctions my intrusion. Pretty May Boyes, if I do not this night advance myself somewhat in your favour it will be an astonishing fact, and no fault of mine."

It was the murmur of female voices which broke upon the ear of Gerald Clifton, and he doubted not for a moment that they proceeded from the room into which the beautiful May Boyes had been conveyed.

An exclamation of surprise arose from someone at his entrance, and then a scream from someone else produced universal confusion among the inmates of the chamber.

But Gerald Clifton was intent upon his purpose, and little he heeded what might be thought or what might be said by others. On the bed, partially covered by its ample coverlet, lay May Boyes, her hair dishevelled, her face pale, and apparently far, very far, from recovered from the mental shock she had so recently received. For the bold intruder to spring to her side was the work of a moment.

"He lives—he lives !" he cried. "May, look up, he lives !"

"My brother ?" half-screamed the beautiful girl.

"Yes, Ratchley ; and is but little hurt."

It was with a cry of delight that she raised herself partially from the bed, and in the impulse of the moment, as if she could not thank enough him who brought her such gladsome tidings, she flung herself upon the breast of Gerald Clifton, and, while his arms encircled her for a brief moment, a gush of tears relieved her over-laden heart.

In another moment she fell backward again, and then the young man, turning to the astonished ladies, lifted his hat, which he still wore, gracefully from his head.

"Ladies," he said, "place your gentlest construction upon this intrusion ; as I am a gentleman, I meant no wrong in coming hither. I know that my presence here is unsanctioned by custom ; let my excuse be that I brought news of joy to Lady May Boyes. Ladies, adieu !"

And so he turned upon his heel and left the room.

"He lives—he lives !" murmured May, "and in those words I live again. Let me rise ; I am much better now. Where is he ? where is Ratchley ?"

At this moment the sound of many voices, and the trampling of feet in the lower part of the inn announced the arrival of the men bearing the still insensible Ratchley Boyes.

May sprang from the bed, and despite a feeble effort to retain her, rushed from the room, meeting the supporters of that corpse-like form, stiffened in blood, before they had well crossed the threshold of the inn.

She was about to utter some exclamation of terror and surprise at seeing Ratchley so immovable when a voice whispered gently in her ear.

"Hush—hush ! dear May. Believe me, there is no danger ; he lives—on my sacred word, he lives."

It was Gerald Clifton.

"I will be calm," she said—"I will be calm," and she hung heavily upon his arm. "With your assurance that he lives, I can be calm."

"Carry him upstairs," cried Sir John ; "no, I mean downstairs ; that is to say, leave him here— or take him into that room, or this, or something. Great minds are always prompt in danger. Do something, somebody, for Heaven's sake ; and then I'll direct you. This way, this way—no, the other way. That it should come to this !—one of our family covered with snow and bleeding ; the precious blood of the Boyes mixing itself up with sand on the floor of an inn. Run for all the doctors, somebody."

In a clear, audible voice, Gerald Clifton directed that the frozen, blood-stained form of Ratchley Boyes should be conveyed into the ball-room, and then, with a skill and readiness which no one thought him capable of possessing, he proceeded not only to examine the wound, but to use such means as it was possible for him to procure for the recovery to consciousness of his friend Ratchley.

"Bless my heart !" said Sir John, "and the nearest doctor lives a dozen miles off. What's to be done now ? The heir-at-law of the great Boyes family waiting for a surgeon. These people of physic ought always to be following about persons of distinction, in case of being wanted ; but it's always the way with the lower orders, they prefer their own ease and idleness to their most sacred duties."

"Let me have some water," said Gerald Clifton, "and a sponge. I think, Sir John, you may safely trust me, in the absence of the regular practitioner, to do what is requisite here. I have made human maladies my study ; and, moreover, I do not think this is a case which will call largely upon my skill. I want some water and a sponge."

"Yes—yes. Ah ! to be sure," said Sir John. "Water and a sponge ! Run everybody for water, and the rest of you for a sponge."

"I will go," said May. "Both water and sponge are in the room above."

She was holding Ratchley's head, and Gerald Clifton saw she was unwilling to leave the brother she loved so well.

"No ; let me go," he whispered.

Away he started for the apartment which he had at first so great a difficulty in finding.

He rushed up the staircase with rapid strides, and paused for a moment, but guided by the moonlight shining through the latticed windows, made his way towards the door of the apartment.

He was within a few paces of reaching it, when a sudden and fearful yell burst upon his ears.

It seemed more like a shout of some wild animal in mockery of a human cry than aught human, reduced even to the most dire extremity.

Well might Gerald reel and stagger in terror and amazement, and he staggered back but just in time to save himself from a more furious attack than was really made upon him.

With a rush, as if propelled by some unseen power, there came sweeping on a human form along the corridor. To grapple him by the throat was the work of a moment—a brief but furious struggle brought them to the stairhead, and, as if he had been an infant in the hands of a giant, was Gerald Clifton hurled down the whole flight.

All this was the work of a moment.

Those who were attending upon Ratchley heard the singular cry from above, and many had made their way to the foot of the staircase. Among the foremost of them was Sir John, who, indeed, had ascended a few steps, not knowing what he was doing or where he was going.

The consequence, however, of this was that he was immediately encountered by the falling form of Gerald Clifton, and such was the rapidity with which they for a few moments rolled over together, that those around could only look on in speechless wonder as to what was going to happen next.

It was Clifton who, notwithstanding the severe fall he had had, sprang to his feet first, leaving poor Sir John stretched out upon his back, apparently without sense or motion.

Fury was in every look and gesture of Clifton, and every eye followed his as he bent an earnest gaze up the staircase. Something dark appeared a considerable distance up.

Clifton had seen it, and before anyone could make a remark upon the circumstance he drew a small pistol from his pocket and fired it up the stairs.

A sharp cry was heard, but when the sound of the pistol's discharge had ceased nothing was heard; and so intense was the dismay and astonishment which had taken possession of all present that each remained in a fixed attitude except Sir John, who now sat up and was woefully touching his nose, from which drops of blood came drop by drop upon the floor between his feet.

"Great Heaven!" exclaimed May, as she clung to Clifton, for she had rushed from the ball-room upon hearing the pistol-shot; "what has happened? Are this night's terrors never to be done?"

"Yes," said Clifton, "they are over; someone attacked me in the corridor above, and I fell down the staircase. I think I have had my revenge, but am not sure. Let those search who will, I care not."

He turned from the staircase, and May Boyes saw it was with a shudder that he did so, and she suspected that dread had more to do than carelessness with his determination not to proceed up the staircase again.

"I don't see," said Sir John Boyes, "why I should be knocked down and trampled upon under any possible circumstances. I had certainly no idea that society was in such a state, I beg leave to remark. Murder!"

"Forgive me, Sir John, it was unintentional," said Clifton. "May Boyes, I have forgotten something, but will see you to-morrow morning at breakfast in your father's hall. Adieu!" adding in a whisper, "remember me."

Without a word of greeting or adieu to another person, he turned and left the inn, encountering, just upon the threshold, a melancholy cavalcade, made up of all the passengers of the Oxford mail, headed by the guard, with his amiable and peaceable blunderbuss in one hand and his horn at his lips, upon which he blew a long and horrible blast, as if they were knights of old arrived at some castle gate, whose frowning portal looked angrily down upon them.

＊   ＊   ＊   ＊   ＊

A week has elapsed, the snow has melted off the heath, one of those sudden and delicious changes has taken place in the aspect of the season which speak to all hearts gently and sweetly of the coming summer.

It was a day suggestive of thoughts of deep sunshine, many-tinted and fragrant flowers, songs of birds, and all those sights and sounds which make the vernal season such a dream of delight.

It was on such an eve as this, one little hour before the coming shadows of the night would envelop all objects, that two figures stood upon a raised terrace which ran along the southern side of Boyes Hall.

The gardens of Boyes Hall were laid out in that style, half formal, half picturesque, which is ascribed to the Italian school.

One of those forms was that of a man, not tall, but of that middle height and symmetrical proportion which betokens more agility than brutal strength.

His companion is young and beautiful, her hands are locked around one of his, while his disengaged arm encircles that slender waist so seeming fragile: and they are not looking on the gardens or the glowing sunset; his eyes are fixed with searching earnestness upon her face, while hers, in downcast, maiden meditation, seem but to see the marble flags upon which they stand.

It is Gerald Clifton—bold, handsome, and full of talent—who has stolen out at this sweet evening hour to whisper such a tale to May Boyes as may well make her ears tingle with delight, and her young heart to beat as though it would burst its dwelling-place.

She loves him! She loves him with such love as a being of such sensibility and intelligence alone can feel.

And did he return with like affection that young girl's happier, better feelings?

Was he the man to feel for her that torrent of blessed emotion which she deserved, as but a fit recompense for the soul-absorbing tenderness in which she held him?

Let us listen to the lovers.

It was Gerald Clifton who spoke, after the silence which had been maintained for nearly the fourth part of an hour; he spoke, too, with enthusiasm, and in that rich, glossy tone which we will not say always masks hypocrisy, but which clever hypocrisy is never without.

"I have long loved you," he said; "since first

I saw you here on this terrace, when your brother and I returned from Oxford at the period of our last happy sojourn in this, to me, sacred and sainted house, I loved you. I loved you, May, from the first not better than I love you now, and now I love you not the less because I feel that heart responds to heart. Is it not so, my sweet May?"

"Gerald Clifton!" was all May could say, and then she seemed to be rather communing with herself, and repeating to her own heart that name which for her bore about it the halo of a magic spell.

There was a silence now again for a few moments' duration, and again Gerald spoke.

"Can you be mine," he said, "knowing so little of me; feeling, even, that the shroud of mystery is around me? Can you yet be mine?"

"For ever!"

"Bold words, May; and yet such as I should not quarrel with. I never loved before I saw you."

"It is destiny," said May. "Let us walk upon the terrace."

"Yes, yes, it may be destiny. We will walk; the air grows chill."

"I felt it not. I knew not that it touched my cheek."

"And, so, May, despite of all your father's anger, perchance, and malediction, a mother's tears, and a brother's fury, you will yet be mine?"

"In my thoughts of you, Gerald Clifton, I have no father, no mother, no brother. 'Tis you who can make or who can destroy me! I am yours, yours only! To live, or to die, to joy, or to suffer I say again, it is my destiny!"

"A strange feeling, May, and yet so closely bordering on my own, for I am not one to make a superstitious clamour of it—I do despair, dearest, of your friends' sanction to our union."

"Then," said May, "our union must want our friends' sanction. What are friends to me?"

"You are young, and you are enthusiastic; as yet you have not known the pressure of a single want. What if I am poor?"

"I care not. We'll live as live the forest birds."

"Nay, May Boyes, you know not that great world of which you speak. But if we fly from here, surely we might take with us something?"

"Yes," said May, "a mutual love, scorning all things but itself."

"Nay, I hear your family have jewels.'

"We have one of priceless lustre."

"Indeed!"

"Yes, in our hearts—fit casket for such a treasure."

"Yes—oh! yes," said Gerald Clifton. "But can we live on air or herbs, on flowers, or on romance?"

"We can beg," May replied.

"A most unsentimental employment," Clifton returned, with sarcasm ringing in his voice. "Why do we talk thus? There is much treasure in this house, but compared to our affections we value it as dross. Yet how glad we should be to have the power of holding out the hand of friendship to deep distress."

"Now I know your motive," said May; "but it must not be. We will touch nothing. Friendless, penniless, if it must be so, we will go forth. I would not lay my hand upon that Indian cabinet or its contents to save my life."

"Perhaps, after all, it contains nothing," Clifton observed, musingly, "but such curiosities as old folks dote upon."

"You are wrong, dear Gerald. But this is a subject scarcely worth discussing."

"True, except out of pure, and, I hope, pardonable inquisitiveness. There is wealth, you say, in the Indian cabinet?"

"A large amount," May replied. "One of our ancestors was a collector of precious stones—indeed, he expended nearly all his income on procuring them. He died, and as he left an estate completely unencumbered, the next heir allowed the jewels to remain, and the next, which is my father, holds possession of them."

"Let us change the subject," said Gerald Clifton. "Dearest May, if I could but find words to tell you how I love you!"

"No words are required," May replied. "When I meet you, look upon me as you do now, and I shall be content. We must part now. I am about to visit Ratchley, and will pass into the house by the picture-gallery. Gerald Clifton, come weal, come woe, I will love you."

She suddenly paused and trembled.

Gerald flew to her side.

"You're unwell," he said, anxiously. "Your colour flits like the sunshine of an April day."

"A sudden pang," she said; "from what cause I know not—'tis over, and all is well. Farewell, until a few short hours, and then joy again. It will be night till then."

She walked slowly down the terrace until she came to a deep bay window, through which she passed into the picture-gallery.

Gerald Clifton gazed after her, musingly; his brows contracted, and he compressed his lips as if he feared to give utterance, even to the idling evening air, to his thoughts.

He muttered something, but so inaudibly that the words were not half formed, and then he turned off in another direction and entered the house.

CHAPTER V.

THE BROTHER AND SISTER.

WE will follow Lady May Boyes to her brother's room.

Although the wound which her brother Ratchley had received was by no means a serious one in itself yet the consequences which had ensued upon it had been of a character to excite serious alarm.

He was a young man in the prime of health and vigour.

He had ridden hard to be present as early as possible at the ball, and his blood was heated and fevered when he received the wound from the highwayman's pistol bullet.

"Well, he didn't go for to do it, you may depend, sir," added a third.

Campbell was furious, and broke away from them with a howl of rage and pain, just managing to see the way to his own office, where it was his duty to sit up all night to receive the reports of the river police, of which he had the control.

. . . . . .

The morning was stealing on apace.

A bright and a beautiful morning it was too, for the storm of the preceding night had chased away the clouds, and imparted a balmy freshness to the air.

The sun shone upon the walls of Newgate, gliding even their rough outlines with beauty.

Adam Beech was roughly awakened from an uneasy slumber into which he had fallen as the morning came.

It was necessary that he should be conveyed to a police office, in order to be regularly committed for trial on the charge of murdering the police-officer.

A course and scanty breakfast was given to him, which he partook in sullen silence.

There were evident appearances of deep mental suffering upon his brow.

No one could pass such a night as he had passed without feeling most acutely its effects.

"Why, what's the matter with you?" said one of the turnkeys to him; "you look as if you had seen something in the night."

"I have," Adam Beech replied, hoarsely.

"The deuce you have! What was it like?"

Beech shuddered; but he made no reply.

It would, indeed, have been too long a tale to tell to any casual inquirer what he had seen, or thought he saw, within the narrow precincts of his dungeon during that most dreadful night.

And now the hour had come when the officer who had charge of Adam Beech thought it necessary to proceed with him to Bow-street, and accordingly he hurried him to depart.

Adam was carefully and securely handcuffed, for the officer was not without his suspicions that the mild and apparently subdued manner of his prisoner might, after all, be only a cloak for some fierce and terrible design that might be productive of much mischief to others, even if it did not succeed in procuring the escape of Adam Beech.

This was a supposition not at all of an improbable nature; the desperate character of the individual was well known, and if, as was most probably the case, he really contemplated his escape, it would be but natural for him, in the first instance, to adopt some course of conduct calculated to dispel suspicion.

The officers set themselves diligently to work to counteract any meditated escape on the part of their prisoner; but, although with an ingenuity that did them infinite credit they thought of a number of possible schemes which he might put in practice, they could be certain of none of them.

They well knew, however, that all the interior arrangements of Newgate were as well-known to professional highwaymen, housebreakers, and other disturbers of public morals, as they were to the official persons intimately connected with those arrangements.

They did not conduct Beech to the vestibule of Newgate by the ordinary route, but in a circuitous manner, through a number of narrow unfrequented passages, upon the walls of which had collected damp of many years, and the atmosphere of which was dark and heavy with unwholesome exhalations.

Now they arrived at the bottom of a flight of stone stairs, which seemed to ascend from those subterraneous regions where they had been wandering to the ordinary level of the prison.

These stairs were set at a steep angle, and Adam Beech mechanically ascended them after stumbling against the first one, so busy was he with the cares of thought which filled his disturbed brain that he scarcely heeded the alteration of movement.

The stone stairs were about fifty in number; and terminated upon a narrow landing, not much more than sufficient for the prisoner and his conductors to stand upon.

Any bold and daring man, caring nothing for personal consequences, might there have obtained a frightful victory over his captors; any struggle upon that confined spot must have immediately precipitated the whole party down the staircase, which, at a glance from above, resembled some dark and deep abyss, the extent of which could only be a subject of conjecture or of a frightful momentary knowledge to any mangled wretch who might reach its bottom to expire.

Some feeling of the peril of such a situation must have crossed the mind of one of the officers, for he made rapid and agitated efforts to unlock a door which immediately faced the head of the stairs, and which certainly was not removed a greater distance than three feet from the topmost step.

"Confound the lock!" he muttered, "if I had given it a thought it should have been open ready for use."

"I could have opened it," said his companion, "had I known you were coming this way; but I did not think it, for this door leads into the stone-room—you know what sort of a lodger there is there?"

"Yes," said the other. "It did not strike me before. The governor ordered the body of the dead woman and child to be laid in that room. We can't go back now—come on."

"Well, there is one comfort," muttered the other, "we've no further to go. I am half-choked with the damp air; give me the key and let me have a try at the lock."

"No—no; wait a bit, I have got it now, it's only rusted in—there, that's right, and a troublesome job it's been this way."

They had been up to this moment carrying a light, for the passages they had traversed were, with very few exceptions, enveloped in profound darkness; but now that door was opened a sudden blaze of daylight burst upon them.

The room was really what might be called a dark one, but the contrast between it and the gloomy passages which Adam Beech had so recently left made it appear to be flooded with light.

Sir John Boyes had been the most curious of the whole family for a description of the man who had attacked his son, but Ratchley answered him distantly, merely saying that the man who had attacked him was a highwayman, and that further he could say nothing.

It was May Boyes alone who seemed to read her brother—to know that there was surely some secret connected with the mode and manner of the attack upon him.

She did not long to know, but yet she had a feeling as if it would have much gratified her to be made acquainted with its minutest particulars.

Noiselessly she entered the sick chamber.

Ratchley was sleeping, and she placed a chair by the bedside, on which she sank to watch his repose.

Ratchley's sleep was anything but profound; moans and impatient murmurs came from his lips, and at times he tossed his arms to and fro, saying, as he did so—

"Off—off—off, murderer—off!"

May watched him intently, and believing that a sleep like that could be in no way refreshing she gently awakened him, and held his hand in both of hers.

"Ratchley—Ratchley, awake," she whispered, softly; "'tis I—your sister, May. What visions are those that disturb your slumbers?"

He gazed upon her for a moment in silence, and then, in a low voice, he spoke—

"Have I been talking, May?" he asked. "What have I been saying?"

"Nothing reasonable, Ratchley—nothing that the judgment could come to any conclusion from."

"It is well—it is well," he said. "Oh! that I were off this bed of pain and suffering. Where is Gerald Clifton?"

"In the house, brother—an honoured guest, for your sake, as well as for his own."

"Sister," said Ratchley, "are we quite alone?"

"Yes—yes. What would you say?"

"It is a secret which I thought to hide deep in the recesses of my heart until I could meet the man of whom I am now about to speak hand to hand."

"What means this preparation? Speak, freely, Ratchley, and at once, to me."

"Before I go further, sister May, answer me some questions. I fancied that during our last vacation you had a liking for this Gerald Clifton, my college friend; but whether that has proved fleeting, or has deepened, I know it will not prevent you answering me truly that which I shall ask of you."

"It will not," said May, in so low a voice that it scarcely reached her brother's ears.

"Then does Gerald Clifton pass his evenings with the family?"

"No, brother. He has a sick friend some miles off, and let the weather be what it may—hail, rain, sleet, or snow—let the loudest wind that ever howled be blowing, he mounts his horse and goes upon his errand of mercy. Is it not great and noble of him?"

"Very," said Ratchley.

"That very," said May, "does not sound like an affirmation of the sentiment. Beware, brother! Breathe not a word of evil against Gerald Clifton.'

"Why beware, May?"

"Because it is impossible you should be right."

"Alas! my sister, this is blind faith—intolerant bigotry," Ratchley said. "I am not strong enough to carry on a long discourse; but beneath yon table lies a small valise; some two hours since it was brought to me by our faithful servant, Andrew. For the first time he found it unlocked in Gerald Clifton's chamber."

"Brother!" exclaimed May, "do I hear aright or is this some dream? Is not Gerald Clifton our guest, and has anyone, knowing him to be such dared so far to violate the rights of hospitality, as to pry into that which alone belongs to him?"

"Hush! sister, hush!" said Ratchley. "You take too romantic a view of this business. It remains yet to be seen who has violated the rights of hospitality—honest Andrew, who has acted under my directions, or Gerald Clifton."

"What mean you?" May cried. "What hideous mummery is this? Brother—brother, you know not what you say."

"Open the valise and look at its contents."

"Never!"

"This is infatuation," Ratchley cried, impatiently. "In that valise is a suit of clothing I have seen before; or, at all events, one of a similar pattern. A scarlet coat, richly trimmed, horseman's boots, lightly made, a hat looped with a jewel, the arms and the accoutrements of him who—"

"What—what, brother—what? Is this a time to pause?"

"It is not—I will finish—who shot me on the heath."

A wild laugh came from May Boyes' lips.

"This is madness," she said—"this is madness! rank insanity—the delirium of fever. Oh! Ratchley—Ratchley, speak of this to none but me."

"Ah! I perceive but too truly," said Ratchley, "that you have warmed this serpent in your bosom but to sting you."

"Serpent!"

"Yes, May. I tell you now I have a s——g notion that it was Gerald Clifton who stepped me on the heath. Hush! sister, not a wo——no a word till I am up and stirring; but keep you an eye upon him for my sake—for your own sake, and for the sake of all you love that are in this house. I tell you, sister, that man is not what he seems."

May Boyes sat for some moments motionless as a statue.

"Oh! yes, I will watch him," she said, as she rose and reeled towards the door. "Who will watch him as I shall? Gerald Clifton—Gerald Clifton, this of thee!"

She reached her own chamber, she clasped her brow for a moment, and then she wrung her hands.

"No—no—no!" she cried "Hush—hush! if it be so it is my destiny. I love him so."

She dashed a quantity of cold water upon her face.

She was death-like pale as she mechanically

arranged the long tresses of her silk-like hair, and then she walked down to the principal hall, where well she knew that Gerald Clifton was wont to linger ere he went on his nightly mission.

Sir John and his lady were in the hall, and Philippa, as well as Gerald Clifton, who was smiling in his own fascinating way.

"Ah! May," he said, "I'm off again. My poor friend is no better. Adieu—adieu! we shall meet in the morning; or, perchance, I may be in early."

May gave him her hand, but the smile with which she accompanied it was forced and painful.

In the hurry of the adieu he did not notice it, and in another moment he had mounted his horse, and was trotting slowly down the avenue of ancient trees that led to the lodge gates.

May slipped out of the room as soon as possible.

The words of her brother had fallen like molten lead upon her brain.

She intended to prove him wrong before she slept that night; at least, so she told herself.

The idea of verifying them never for a moment crossed her imagination.

With a quick, light step she went to the stables of the mansion. Her own favourite horse was reposing in its stall.

She sought no idle, lounging groom, but, with her own hands, as quick as thought, she harnessed her steed, and in a few minutes she was away.

A hazardous leap took her into a meadow, a hard gallop across its surface brought her to a point beyond the lodge gates, and there she paused; both horse and rider were still, as if sculptured, to watch Gerald Clifton.

Hark! he comes.

She pressed her hands upon her throbbing bosom to still its tumultuous beating.

He comes—he comes! Him in whom her very existence was centred—he comes!

She heard the sound of his horse's feet; there was to her heart a magic in the very tread of the animal who bore him.

In the dim and dusky eve she saw him; he passed, all was still, save the solemn tread of the horse's feet upon the hardened ground.

She scarcely breathed till he had passed some distance.

"On—on!" she cried, to her horse; and like the wind she skirted the road across the meadows, and made a rapid detour.

She felt that, at the pace she had been going, she must be far ahead of him again, and then she paused, horse and rider motionless as before.

Oh! what a dreadful chase was that for such a heart as was then wildly beating in the bosom of poor May Boyes.

Heaven help her then! Alas! she had much need of its assistance.

Breathless again—and still again, as a painted horse and a painted rider, they stood.

Again he came on.

He had increased his pace to a trot; and as he neared her, the trot became a canter. Faster—faster still he came on, and now he swept by most rapidly.

"A chase—a chase!" she cried. "Let it lead me where it will, I'll join it."

She cleared the hedge, and put her horse to a gallop.

Pursued and pursuer were now on the heath.

Surely some evidence of what was following so hard upon his track had reached Gerald Clifton's mind, for his fleet horse was put to its utmost pace, and, for a time, he was gaining rapidly.

A kind of madness seized on May.

By voice and gesture she urged that favourite palfrey to a perfect fury.

The hot breath steamed from his dilated nostrils, foam gathered at his mouth, and drop by drop the heavy perspiration reeked from its sides.

But never did a wild steed carry a wild rider with more fearful velocity, over hillock and glen, or brake, bush, and brier, than did the favoured horse carry its fearless burden.

And now she paused again, breathless and motionless as a statue, until Gerald should again reach the spot, which she knew he must pass.

She felt a conviction that she had distanced him, and that, in the gloom of the evening, she had far out-stripped even the headlong progress of his wild, daring steed.

She could feel the palpitation of her own heart, and, to her perception, that sounded louder than the tramp of Gerald Clifton's horse's feet, as now she felt assured that he was in advance.

Did she really wish now that Gerald Clifton should see her?

It would almost seem as if she did, for still and statue-like she stood in his very path.

But he was sweeping onward, and his chief attention was directed to what sounds might come upon his track behind.

The thought that he was pursued had once found a place in his heart, and now the most trivial sounds that came upon the night air were, to his imagination, full of danger, and the heralds of capture, and, perchance, of death.

And so was it that he came upon the form of the young girl so suddenly and unawares that it appeared to him as if from the very night air around her she had sprung into existence, and stood there like some warning spectre to turn him from his path.

The sudden movement he gave to the rein of his steed imparted terror to the animal—for no living creature is so soon aware of its master's fears or hesitation as the horse.

Alas! had he stayed he might have had a blessing, and not for one brief moment did he pause, except to battle with his steed and to dash away the sudden gush of perspiration that broke out upon his brow, as he made a complete circuit to avoid what he considered the spectral appearance which seemed to stay his path.

Then May Boyes smote her hands.

"He does not love me!" she cried—"he does not love me. Just Heaven! there must be a victim. Heaven grant that I may be born to suffer, not avenge. On—on—on!"

Clifton was now far distant.

Terror had added speed to the flight of his horse.

He had plunged the spurs rowel-deep in the before sufficiently goaded animal's flanks.

Again he heard his wild pursuer speeding on.

"Confusion!" he cried; "there are but two beings this night on Hounslow-heath—myself and some demon who would chase me to the gallows! Oh! for the shelter of the hut, oh! for bars and bolts to keep the grim intruder out. I shake in every limb. What fiend is this that chases me across the heath?"

With lips pale and compressed, eyes preternaturally fixed and open, and the damp hair hanging about his brows, Gerald Clifton at length arrived at the thick plantation, nearly in the centre of which was the hut where the highwayman so short a time had halted for change of raiment and refreshment.

Need we attempt to keep a secret our readers have already guessed?—that the knight of the road and the accomplished Gerald Clifton, the lover of the beautiful May Boyes, the almost murderer of her brother, the winner of all hearts, the graceful, the gay, the witty, and the intelligent, are—one!

Conviction surely must have reached May Boyes now.

Could she longer doubt? Was there a suspicion of her brother now unverified?

Not one, if she could have suffered her heart to obey its soberer dictates.

But yet she would see with her own eyes further evidence that Gerald Clifton's was the arm which had been raised against her brother's life.

She saw his form disappear on the precincts of the wood, and, ere she was aware, she reached a point where stood his panting steed tied to the overhanging limb of an aged beech, while its master, on foot, was threading the intricacies of the plantation.

"Here will I pause," she said, "and wait for him."

How long she waited she knew not.

The biting cold affected her not—she felt not the keen breeze that now blew across the heath, for, as the night advanced, stern winter once again seemed to have assumed his sceptre, and to have swept from off the earth's fair surface all those gladsome indications of the coming spring.

And what had promised to become a gentle rain now descended in slow flakes, mingled with sharper icy particles; but still she waited. Ay! and until the break of dawn would she have waited there, if human nature could have supported her, rather than not see Gerald Clifton as he should come back again.

And now her straining ears catch the sound of some hasty footsteps, and she knew that he was coming. This, indeed, was a crisis to her fate.

How would he come, and what appearance would he bear? Would the idol of her heart be changed, or would he wear the self-same aspect that he wore?—momentous question. If back he came the Gerald Clifton that he went, unchanged in outward seeming, she might be happy yet.

But, hark! nearer, nearer he comes, and now she hears his voice.

His courage is returned—the brief attack of horror he has shaken off—the courage and the daring of the wine-cup is now in him.

She hears his voice, she knows it is his voice; but, oh! it is not the voice that has spoken to her in the low, soft accents of affection. No, no! no more is he the Gerald Clifton of her dreams.

"Great Heaven!" she exclaimed, "I loved an angel—he has become a man."

A ribald song was coming from his lips, such a half-tipsy laugh as might have graced the purlieus of St. Giles's.

She heard him emphasis the coarser jests with which it teemed; and now forth he came into the dim light, by which she could observe him. Oh, what a change was there!

We have already described to our readers the dashing highwayman, the foppery of his half military costume, the elaborate decoration, and the brilliant colouring of his clothing, the assumption of a desire to shine in his iniquity, and to affect its being a fancy pursuit, to require an elaboration of toilet to set it out.

Our readers know all this, but it was new to poor May Boyes.

She saw him tighten the saddle-girths, she heard him talk to the horse, and then she saw him mount.

She could not speak, but she stretched forth her arms. She felt at that moment that she must for ever loathe him, or for ever love him.

The scales hung even, and then surely some evil spirit whispered him to make disgust kick the beam. He paused a moment ere he galloped to the heath, and with one of those old and well-remembered sighs, that ever seemed to come from the very bottom of a heart replete with the best and noblest of the human sympathies, he said—

"Poor May Boyes! I am sorry that she loves me; she deserves a better fate."

In an instant he was gone.

"Gerald—Gerald!" cried May. "Gerald Clifton yet a moment! turn, Gerald, turn. He is gone. Oh, Heaven! where are your friendly lightnings now? Here, at least, is a head that will not shrink from the fell stroke. Gerald Clifton—Gerald Clifton, I love you! yes, I love you still."

She dropped her head upon the neck of her steed, tears fell fast from those sweet eyes that were proverbial through the county for their laughing joy.

Her heart was breaking—the night of her destiny had come.

Never, never again would the sun of joy illumine the best and dearest heart that ever beat in human bosom.

CHAPTER VI.

AN ACTIVE-MINDED MAGISTRATE.

SIR JOHN BOYES sat in great state that night in his own hall.

The eccentric combination of notions which he called his mind was uncommonly severe, and from about mid-day had been extremely dictatorial.

The fact is, he had been dreadfully alarmed at Ratchley's situation, but now that he had been assured by a cunning leech, whom he looked upon as a kind of Solomon in the physical way, to use an expression of his own, of the certain convalescence of the young man, Sir John had dismissed all his fears, and continually spoke in aphorisms upon the most trifling subject.

He had put on his most elaborate laced cravat, and his fingers were loaded with those family rings that made so graceful a scintillation whenever he imparted to his illustrious hand that tremulous motion for which he was so celebrated.

"Lady Boyes," he said, "upon casting my eyes around this apartment, and observing that our daughter May is not present, I am irresistibly led to the conclusion that she is a—a—in a manner of speaking, somewhere else. Let her be summoned."

The Lady May was summoned, but she came not, and so half an hour more passed away, and Sir John began to get a little fidgety.

The family rings somehow did not look quite so bright, and the faultless tie of the cravat no longer fixed his gaze in the mirror opposite to him, for Sir John always looked at a mirror, and took care to sit in such a position in the room that he had that opportunity.

Moreover, he began to perceive that Lady Boyes went in and out of the room repeatedly with an anxious expression of countenance, so that the idea of there being something amiss began gradually to develop itself through the intellectual fog which generally obscured his perception.

He heard, too, a great deal of running up and down stairs, and finally, when he turned round to address an observation to Philippa, to his astonishment he found that he was left completely alone.

"What's the meaning of this?" he said; "the heir of all the Boyesses left by himself! I never did hear of such a thing in all my life—it's monstrous. Perhaps they expect me to fall back upon my own thoughts, but I can't do it; and my unequivocal opinion is, that when a man's left alone he has not a soul to talk to. Bless my soul, who are you?"

This exclamation arose from the fact that the door was slowly opened, and a strange, rough-looking fellow made his appearance, who, immediately that he saw Sir John observed him, placed his fingers on his lips.

"Hush! don't say anything, old cock," said the man, mysteriously. "Have you any idea where I shall find any of them?"

We certainly feel quite unqualified to present to the reader anything like a literal picture of Sir John's face at this moment.

The idea of anyone walking into his ancestral home, and unannounced getting to him, face to face, and then and there addressing him as an old cock, amounted to a series of extravagant propositions which completely bewildered poor Sir John, and at the same time it induced a belief that the whole framework of society was shattered to pieces.

It completely choked his utterance, so that he could do nothing for some moments but glare at the visitor with something of the singular expression of some great fish newly dragged from his native element into the open air.

"Mum's the word," said the man. "Snug as possible. Eh! is there anybody at home? Why, what's the matter with you?"

"Eh, eh!" said Sir John; "who am I?"

"Well, I don't know, you look like a thundering fool. I want to see Sir John Boyes. What sort of a fellow is he? Active, bold—eh?"

"Where am I?" demanded Sir John, feebly.

"Hang it all," said the man; "is this a lunatic asylum? If it is so, it's very badly guarded, for the deuce a soul I met as I walked in here. But my business won't bear delay—I want to see some of the family."

"I am the family," gasped Sir John. "What do you want here? And how came you into the presence of the thirteenth baronet of this house in such a manner?"

"You!" said the man; "you don't mean to say you're Sir John Boyes?"

"Well, I think I am," said Sir John.

"Really, sir, I beg your pardon!" the man said; "but as I found you sitting here all by yourself, and that anybody might walk in, I couldn't believe it was you. I have come all the way from London to see you. The Secretary of State—you understand—"

"The Secretary of State!" exclaimed Sir John, and he immediately raised his cravat. "Sir, are you a Government messenger?"

"Why, yes, in a manner of speaking, Sir John, I may be called a Government messenger. I'm a runner."

"A what—a rummer, did you say?"

"No; a runner—a Bow-street runner."

"A thief-taker?"

"Precisely, whenever I can catch them. My name's Long, and I'm rather, you see, long by nature. The Secretary of State has received information that Captain Hawk, the highwayman, had been in this district. The fact is, the Oxford mail has been robbed. But there wouldn't have been much fuss about that, only that there happened to be in the mail-bag some correspondence of his lordship which has fallen into the hands of somebody—Heaven knows who; at all events, as it was all through Captain Hawk that the confusion arose, his lordship, after swearing some tremendous oaths, has made up his mind to have him nabbed."

"Oh!" said Sir John, who was rather bewildered at the rapidity with which the Bow-street runner spoke.

"You will, therefore, perceive," Long continued, "why am I down here. Hawk never leaves a district without perpetrating some outrageous robbery by way of leaving a little relic behind him. Now the probability is, that he will take an opportunity of breaking into your house; for, as his lordship says, the greater the goose the greater the danger."

"The greater the what?" said Sir John.

"Oh! never mind that; I want to know if Captain Hawk has been seen in the vicinity?"

"I can't tell you, Mr. Strong," said Sir John.

"I beg your pardon, my name's Long."

"Hang your name, sir, you're an impertinent fellow !"

"Very good, go on," said Long, and he gave his hands such a smack together that Sir John jumped again ; "go on, don't mind me."

"Confound you !" said Sir John, "I never met your equal. There's my son, sir, the representative that will be of the Boyeses, six feet two and a quarter in pumps, and amazingly like the family, has been shot at by this very Captain Hawk ; and I've no objection to offer a hundred—that is to say I mean fifty—or ten pounds, or so, to anybody who will catch him ; but I don't want to have anything to say to you, Mr. Gong."

"Sir John, my name's Long !"

"I don't care what your name is—get out of my house !" Sir John roared. "You may be Long and Strong, and Strong and Long, and Gong too, for what I care."

"Oh ! stuff, stuff, stuff," said the officer, as he threw himself into a chair ; "don't commit yourself."

"Don't do what ?"

"Now, my dear sir—now, my dear sir—"

"Was ever a great Boyes so insulted ?" Sir John roared. "But I'll pretty soon put an end to this ! Hang it, sir, I'll have you thrown in a horsepond and dipped in a blanket !"

Sir John rose as he spoke, and rang the bell violently.

"There he goes again," said the officer, as if he were addressing some other person ; "just the very character I heard of him—an ass to the backbone."

Sir John's summons to the bell was so powerful a one, that not only did he succeed in alarming the whole house, but he brought the rope down in his hand, and there he stood, looking like a maniac, as two or three of the servants rushed into the hall.

"Turn this Mr. Prong out !" said Sir John. "Kick him out ! Am I to be insulted in my own house ? By the bones of my ancestors—kick him out—kick him out !"

"Well," said the officer, rising, "of all the fools that ever I met with at pronouncing a fellow's name, you're about the worst. You know my name's Long, well enough—L-o-n-g, stupid !"

Sir John danced in agony.

"Am I to put up with this ?" he exclaimed. "Is the whole family to put up with this ? Are the Boyeses to be nonentities ? Is this to become a family tale, to be told to the famtly ears ?"

"Oh !" said Long, "you acknowledge to have some asinine appendages, do you ? Come now, Sir John, we'll make it all square over a bottle. I'll forgive you—perhaps it's natural."

"Is the fellow to be turned out or is he not ?" shrieked Sir John.

There were two or three stout serving men who had entered the apartment ; and now that they had really got over their first surprise at the astonishing impertinence of the stranger, they flung themselves upon him, and lifting him up bodily, carried him from the room.

"Thank you—thank you," said the imperturbable Mr. Long. "Now this is kind—easy there, mind that corner. Bye-bye, Sir John ; turn it over in your mind, and I'll look in again in an hour. As for all of you, my good fellows, you'll find a jug of ale apiece at the Talbot. Never forget, whatever your master may say, that my name is Long—L-o-n-g, and that I came about Captain Hawk, the celebrated highwayman—remember that, will you ?"

He was flung down the hall steps without much ceremony, whilst Sir John sat puffing like a grampus and in a terrible state of mind.

Never before had his dignity been so insulted ; never before had anybody hinted to him a suspicion that he was not to the full as great a man as he believed himself ; but now to be told to his face that he was an ass—to have the chances of his house being broken into first speculated upon because he was the greatest goose in the country !

He forgot for the moment the anxious search for May ; and at length, when Lady Boyes and Philippa entered the apartment, he was so bewildered that they found him quite incapable of answering, even as rationally as usual, to what might be said to him.

"Oh ! Sir John," said Lady Boyes, "we cannot find May anywhere."

"Hang Strong !" said Sir John.

"We've searched for her," said Philippa, "through the whole house. Ratchley says she was with him about an hour ago, but no one has seen her since."

"That scoundrel Gong !"

"Mother, what is he talking of ?" said Philippa.

"I don't know," said Lady Boyes ; "but I'm afraid his poor wits are gone."

"Poor wits," said Sir John "I wonder what next. Is my own family joining that villain Strong against me ?"

"It is in vain," said Lady Boyes, "to appeal to your father, Philippa ; it is evident he knows not what he says."

"Yes, I do," said Sir John. "There's been a rascal here of the name of Gong, or something of that kind, and he's been insulting me past all bounds of moderation. I can't stand it, and I won't !"

There was a tremendous knocking at the hall door of the mansion, and in a few moments a servant came into the room and said—

"If you please, Sir John, Mr. Long's come back again. He says he's only one observation to make, which he wishes you particularly to hear."

"The devil !" roared Sir John. "Knock him down ! Don't let him into the house on any account—kill him, if you like !"

The servant left the room, and then Sir John wiped the perspiration from his brow with the end of his cravat.

"This is rather too dreadful," he said. "I'll write to the secretary of state to-morrow and claim his protection against Long. What were you saying, Lady Boyes, when you came in ?"

"That our child May has disappeared, Sir John."

"May—May! You don't mean our May Boyes!"

"Alas!" said Lady Boyes, "it is too true."

She sat down and burst into tears, and at the moment she did so the door of the apartment opened, and May, pale as a ghost, glided in.

"What is too true, mother?" she said.

A scream of joy escaped from Lady Boyes, and she flung her arms round her daughter's neck while Philippa clasped her sister's hands and looked all the happiness she felt at her return.

Poor Sir John sat and fidgeted about in the most ludicrous manner.

"I don't understand what you're all about," he said. "Here's been Long, and Strong, and Gong, and Prong, here; and then you set to crying, and then May's gone and May comes. I don't understand it; and I believe I may remark, that when I don't understand anything I don't comprehend it."

"What is it all about?" said May. "I very much fear that heedless ramble I took upon the heath has caused you all disquietude."

"Oh! my child," said Lady Boyes, "how could you go out at such a time and so alarm us?"

"I am very sorry, mother," said May.

"And you look pale, and worn, and ill!" said Philippa. "Tell me, dear May, has anything happened to harass you?"

"Nothing," said May; "all is well. It was careless of me, at such a time, to ramble to the heath; but now you see I'm returned, think nothing of it. I have some letters to write, and shall be in my own room an hour or more."

She smiled as she spoke, and left the room.

"Let her be," said Lady Boyes. "Of late I have observed that these melancholy moods have seized upon her; 'tis best to leave her to herself, for I have found that she recovers more quickly and more completely."

"Very good," said Sir John; "but I don't see why anybody should be melancholy but me."

"I will go to the library," he added, "and endeavour to quiet my nerves by consulting the works of one of those great of men antiquity who remind me so much of myself. I always feel like Julius Cæsar—don't let me be disturbed unless I ring."

So saying, and having recovered a good deal of his solemn gravity, Sir John rose, and took a small lamp from a side table; but, before he could reach the door of the apartment, it was opened again, and one of the servants stood in a very hesitating manner upon the threshold.

"I beg your pardon, Sir John," he said, and then he paused.

"What is it?" said Sir John. "Speak freely, my man—what is it?"

"Why, Sir John, I hope you won't be offended with me—but—but—"

"Will you have the goodness to explain your errand? Is the representative of one of the oldest baronetcies in this country to be kept waiting your leisure?"

"Certainly not, Sir John. I only beg your pardon! but since your worship gives me leave to speak, I've come to say that Mr. Long has come again and he says—"

"Fire and fury!" said Sir John; "when is this Long persecution to end? Am I to be bull-baited here by a Long? Am I a badger—that's what I ask you all—am I badger, Lady Boyes—do you take me for a badger?"

"Beg pardon, Sir John," said the servant; "I thought you'd be angry, sir, but really, sir, Mr. Long is so civil, and such a gentlemanly man, that we hardly knew him again. Of course, Sir John, we kept him outside till your pleasure was known."

"A thousand devils!" said Sir John. "Hang his civility! souse him with buckets of water, and then thrash him off the premises!—I'll hold you harmless of the consequence."

"Yes, Sir John, if it's your pleasure; but he says he comes from the Secretary of State."

"I know it, the hardened ruffian! Hang the Secretary of State and him, too! Do as I bid you, or I'll turn every man of you out of the house!"

The servant went his way, and from the general confusion which ensued it may well be presumed that Sir John's instructions were amply carried out, and that the unfortunate Long at length met with a due reward for his impertinence.

Such folks as Sir John Boyes have always a sufficient fund of personal vanity to draw upon under any emergency, and therefore it was that he so easily got over the effects of the highly injurious expressions used by that impertinent Long when talking of his, Sir John's, mental endowments.

He went to the library and sat down quite in a comparatively amiable frame of mind, and it so happened that he sat directly opposite to one of the windows.

He reached a volume from one of the shelves and commenced reading, fancying that he fully understood the author's meaning, looking exceedingly pompous the while, and occasionally tapping the front of his forehead, as if to give a hint to any part of his intellectual organisation which might be slumbering that he fully expected it to be up and at work.

"Ah!" he exclaimed, "that is precisely my opinion. It is an astonishing fact how, from age to age, and from period to period, when great minds commence a course of—of rational thought, how they continually go on, in a manner of speaking—that is to say, from age to age, and from period to period."

Sir John looked up at the ceiling, as if he had uttered something profound; but he was soon recalled from this formidable metaphysical flight by a noise at the window opposite to which he sat.

Sir John's mouth opened to an alarming width, and so did his eyes, as one-half of the window swung gently into the room upon its hinges, and a figure appeared, such as he had never seen before, but of which common report had frequently given him rather an accurate description.

There was the scarlet coat, trimmed with rich lace, the costly cravat, the riding-boots, the hat and feather, looped with a diamond, all the insignia complete of no less a personage than the celebrated Captain Hawk, the highwayman.